JEASY   4/03

Wollman, Jessica.

Andrew's bright blue
T-shirt /
c2002.

Andrew's Bright Blue T-shirt

Story by **Jessica Wollman**
Pictures by **Ana López Escrivá**

A Doubleday Book for Young Readers

For Dan
—J.W.

A Doubleday Book for Young Readers

Published by Random House Children's Books
a division of
Random House, Inc.
1540 Broadway
New York, New York 10036

Visit us on the Web! www.randomhouse.com/kids
Educators and librarians, for a variety of teaching tools, visit us at www.randomhouse.com/teachers

Cataloging-in-Publication Data is available from the Library of Congress.
ISBN 0-385-74616-4 (trade)   0-385-90853-9 (lib. bdg.)

The text of this book is set in 17-point Rotis Sans Serif.

Book design by Liney Li

Manufactured in the United States of America

October 2002

10 9 8 7 6 5 4 3 2 1

Andrew loved his bright blue T-shirt.

It used to belong to his older brother, Ernie. But when Ernie grew too big to wear it, he gave it to Andrew. Andrew was just the right size for it. As soon as he tried it on, he knew that it would *always* be his favorite shirt.

He loved the cool bright blue and the picture of the soccer ball on the front.

Andrew had never played soccer, but he watched Ernie and his friends play all the time. Ernie always said that Andrew was too little to join them, but Andrew knew that someday he'd be big enough.

Andrew wore the T-shirt every day.

He slept in it.

He played in it.

He wore it when he went grocery shopping with his mom.

He wore it when he and his dad made spaghetti and meatballs.

He wore it in the summer to his uncle Jim and aunt Helen's Fourth of July picnic.

He even wore it on lazy days when he wasn't doing much of anything.

Andrew wore his blue T-shirt so much that people started to notice.

When school started in the fall, Andrew's teacher called him Bright Blue Andrew. This made Andrew smile.

Every time he got on the school bus, the driver said, "Hello, blue-shirt boy." This made Andrew giggle.

Some people didn't think Andrew's T-shirt was so great.

"You know, it's not very healthy to wear the same dirty T-shirt over and over again," said his mother.

"Why are you wearing a soccer T-shirt if you don't know how to play soccer?" asked his sister.

"If you keep on wearing that shirt every day, it'll stick to

your skin and you'll *never* be able to get it off," teased his brother.

But Andrew didn't pay much attention to them. He did agree to take off his shirt every few days so that his mom could wash it, but other than that, he kept on wearing his cool blue T-shirt everywhere he went.

When winter came, Andrew's classmates dressed differently.
They all wore heavy coats, long pants, and thick sweaters.
Andrew also wore a heavy coat and long pants.
But he refused to change his bright blue T-shirt.

One morning, Andrew noticed that his T-shirt felt a little tight under his arms. He tried to stretch it by making big circles in the air. But the shirt still felt a wee bit small.

All day in school, Andrew tried to stretch out his T-shirt.

He tugged at it during lunch.

He twisted it during story time.

But by the end of the day, his bright blue T-shirt still felt tight. It started to feel tight *every* day.

It got harder and harder to pull his shirt on every morning. The holes for his arms and head just seemed to be getting smaller and smaller.

Then one morning, Andrew looked down and noticed that his belly was poking out from underneath his shirt.

He could even see his belly button!
Andrew tried to pull the shirt down, but no matter how hard he pulled, it refused to cover his tummy.

People started to notice.

"Why does your shirt look so funny?" asked his sister as she wrinkled up her nose.

Andrew pretended not to hear her.

"I think it's time to find a new favorite T-shirt," said his dad during dinner.

Andrew shoved an entire meatball into his mouth and replied, "Hmmrph."

"Maybe you should put your T-shirt on that dolly you play with," teased his brother.

"Mr. Fuzzball is *not* a dolly," said Andrew, shaking his head. "He's a bear."

Finally, Andrew's mom took him shopping. She let him pick out a pair of green pants and a bright orange ski jacket. But when she asked him to pick out a new shirt, he refused. Andrew loved his bright blue T-shirt.

His mother bought him some new shirts anyway. Andrew
put them in the very back of his closet, where he kept all his
broken toys.

In the spring, the snow melted and Ernie and his friends played soccer every day after school.

Andrew watched and tried to memorize all their special moves. When Ernie wasn't home, Andrew practiced dribbling, blocking, and kicking . . . over and over again.

One afternoon, Andrew was watching Ernie and his friends play soccer, when suddenly . . . Ernie kicked the ball out of bounds. It landed right in front of Andrew.

Without even thinking, Andrew pulled his leg back and kicked the ball—hard. It sailed straight through the air and landed at Ernie's feet.

Ernie didn't touch the ball.

None of his friends moved.

Everybody stared at Andrew.

Andrew's cheeks turned bright red and he stared at the
ground.

"Wow!" shouted Ernie. "That was a *great* kick."

Ernie's friends nodded.

Andrew's cheeks turned even redder. "It was?" he asked as Ernie walked toward him.

Ernie looked at Andrew and smiled. He looked at Andrew's T-shirt and smiled again.

"I mean, I knew you'd gotten *bigger*," he said. "But I didn't know you'd gotten *stronger*."

Andrew thought about this. He understood that being big was not the same as being strong. His block buildings were big, but they certainly weren't strong. Being big was good, and being strong—well, that was even better. But being big *and* strong, that was the absolute best.

Andrew looked at his arms again and made a muscle—a *huge* muscle.

Andrew looked down at his legs. Maybe they did look a little longer.

Ernie was right. He *had* gotten bigger and stronger. How had he not noticed this before?

Ernie stared at Andrew's muscle. He looked impressed. "Hey, we could use another player. Do you want to be on my team?"

Andrew looked at Ernie's friends. They were smiling at him.

Andrew smiled back and giggled. "Sure," he said. "That'll be fun."

Then Andrew looked down at his tiny blue T-shirt. His big, strong arms suddenly didn't feel so comfortable. His big, strong tummy was poking out, too.

Andrew knew just what he had to do. "Wait one minute,"
he shouted as he ran into the house. "I'll be right back."

Bernard
THE ANGRY ROOSTER

Mary Wormell

Farrar Straus Giroux • New York

Bernard was a very proud speckled rooster. It was his
job to wake everyone up each morning.
"Cock-a-doodle-doo, good morning to you,
cock-a-doodle-doo."

He spent his day looking after the chickens and he
was happy.

But one day all of this changed. When Lucy brought breakfast for him and the chickens, he started to chase after her.

"What's the matter with you, Bernard?" shouted Lucy,
   as she ran and climbed up onto the fence.
"Why are you so cross?"

But Bernard didn't answer.

When Tommy the ginger cat went to lie in the sun
for his morning nap, Bernard ran and leaped onto
his back.

"What's the matter with you, Bernard?" meowed Tommy,
as he scrambled up a tree. "Why are you so cross?"

But Bernard didn't answer.

Then when Toby the scruffy dog walked past to get
to his lunch, Bernard was still angry and he jumped
at Toby and pecked his tail.

"What's the matter with you, Bernard?" yelped Toby,
as he bounded up onto the straw bales. "Why are you
so cross?"

But Bernard didn't answer.

The chickens couldn't figure out what was wrong with Bernard. "What's the matter with you today?" they all asked together. "Why are you so cross?"

But Bernard didn't answer.

He just ushered the chickens to the other side of
the yard, glancing over his shoulder as he did so.

Then he marched over to where Callum the hairy pony was munching grass and sprang up onto his back.

Callum got such a shock that he bucked as high
as he could. Bernard went spinning up-up-up
through the sky.

"Oh no, he's going to be really angry now," whispered Lucy.
"Who knows what he'll do?" breathed Tommy the ginger cat.
"He'll be even more cross," murmured Toby the scruffy dog.

"That'll teach you to jump on my back," whinnied Callum
the hairy pony.
And when Bernard landed bump on top of the stable roof,
the chickens all gasped, "Ooooh!"

But Bernard didn't look angry. He stood up and shook
himself, then walked over to a tree and began to climb.

When he reached the highest branch, he looked at the
new weather vane on top of the farmhouse and crowed,
"Cock-a-doodle-doo, now I'm higher than you,
cock-a-doodle-doo."

"So that's what's the matter with Bernard!"
exclaimed everyone, as Bernard crowed again,
even louder.

From that day on, everyone was happy, especially
Bernard, who knew he could always be the highest
rooster around—with a little help, of course!

For Lucy and Joan

Copyright © 2001 by Mary Wormell

Distributed in Canada by Douglas & McIntyre Ltd.

Color separations by Hong Kong Scanner Arts

Printed and bound in the United States of America

by Berryville Graphics

Typography by Judy Lanfredi

First edition, 2001

1 3 5 7 9 10 8 6 4 2

Library of Congress Cataloging-in-Publication Data

Wormell, Mary.

    Bernard the angry rooster / Mary Wormell. — 1st ed.

       p.   cm.

    Summary: Bernard the rooster becomes unusually grumpy one day,

causing the other animals to be concerned about his behavior.

    ISBN 0-374-30670-2

    [1. Roosters—Fiction.   2. Domestic Animals—Fiction.]   I. Title.

PZ7.W88774 Be   2001

[E]—dc21   00-35459